"I've got to try the special of the day—the heart-shaped pancakes," JoJo Siwa said, grinning at the waitress as she scribbled away on her notepad. "With strawberries and whipped cream and chocolate sauce." The waitress nodded, offering JoJo a smile. "Oh, and a glass of orange juice, please!"

"I'll have a cup of coffee and the stuffed French toast," Jessalyn Siwa said, closing her menu and placing it on the table.

"Mom, how can you pass up the chance to have heart-shaped pancakes? I mean, they only come around once a year!" JoJo exclaimed as the waitress walked away. "It's almost Valentine's Day! Heart-shaped foods should be eaten as often as possible!"

"Well, technically, Valentine's Day is still almost a month away," Jess replied, laughing. "Plus, I figure I'll just have a bite of yours."

"*If* I let you." JoJo waggled her eyebrows. "I'll probably want them all to myself . . ."

"No problem," Jess said. "That's sort of how I'm feeling about my French toast. Remember French toast? Your favorite breakfast? Don't worry, I'm sure I can handle it on my own."

"Correction: French toast is my favorite when heart-shaped pancakes aren't on the menu! But fine. You win. We'll share." It was a game they always played—but they both always wound up sharing. JoJo knew

CONTENTS

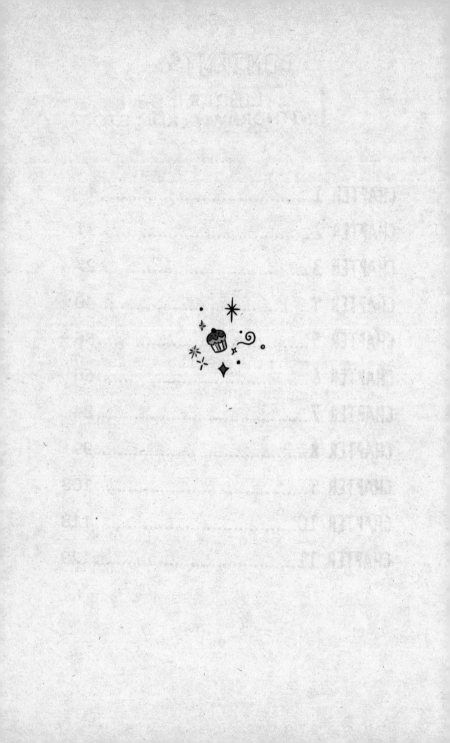

the real reason her mom had ordered the stuffed French toast was because she knew how much JoJo loved it, and she had planned on sharing it with her all along. It was just one of the many things JoJo loved about her mom.

Speaking of love . . . JoJo *loved* Valentine's Day. It was one of her favorite holidays, right up there with Christmas, Halloween, and her birthday. And BowBow's birthday, of course. BowBow was JoJo's adorable teacup Yorkie.

"We should talk about Valentine's Day, actually," Jessalyn said, taking a sip of her water. "Your dance workshop will be ending the day before Valentine's Day, right? It's going to be a very busy few weeks between now and then. Don't forget, we have a showcase scheduled the weekend after Valentine's Day and have to leave the morning of the sixteenth."

"That's right," JoJo replied. "You know, on second thought, I'm in no rush for Valentine's Day to get here. I don't want my class to go by too quickly. I can't believe it's finally about to start! It feels like I auditioned a million years ago . . ." JoJo paused as the waitress came by the table to drop off their beverages. "I'm still so excited I made it into the class!"

"It's definitely an honor to have been selected," Jessalyn agreed as she poured a little milk into her coffee. "But I'm not surprised. You've worked so hard for this."

JoJo had auditioned for the dance workshop back in November. There were only ten spots available in the almost four-week class, which was an immersive, multidisciplinary workshop being taught exclusively for girls by one of the most famous retired female choreographers in the world. Female dancers of all ages, from all over the country, had auditioned to be accepted into the workshop, which was being held in Los Angeles. The spots were awarded on a scholarship basis, which meant the workshop was free to anyone who made it in. JoJo had been thrilled when she was accepted and had been counting down the days until it began. She'd even circled her first day in fluorescent pink marker on her calendar and drawn a bunch of hearts around it. And now the big day was finally here!

"I can't wait to see who else will be in the program," JoJo said, drumming her fingers on the table. "And what kind of dancers they'll be. I remember there were a bunch of classically trained ballerinas at the audition. I hope some of them made it in—it would be so cool to be dancing alongside actual professional ballerinas!"

5

JoJo had plenty of experience with dance classes, since she'd been performing pretty much her whole life—first for fun and now professionally. She'd gotten an extra-early start, dancing onstage for the first time when she was only two years old! JoJo always felt right at home in a dance class and couldn't wait to meet the other dancers in the workshop. She was sure it was going to be one of the most exciting opportunities of her life.

"I bet there will be dancers from all disciplines," Jessalyn said, sipping her coffee. "And I also wouldn't be surprised if you are one of the youngest dancers in the workshop, if not *the* youngest." Her mom put her mug down. "It's a good thing you're used to being the youngest one in the group!"

"True." JoJo nodded. "I'm always up for making new friends and adding some big sisters to my dance family." Her eyes twinkled, and she bounced in her seat. She was so excited, it was hard to sit still!

Just then, the waitress appeared at the table and plunked down two heavy plates. Jessalyn's plate held two giant pieces of French toast sprinkled with powdered sugar and oozing maple syrup, but JoJo's plate was nothing short of spectacular. JoJo inhaled the wonderful, sweet scent of pancakes and admired the perfect heart-shaped stack loaded with strawberries and fudge sauce. Her stomach growled at the sight.

"I have to take a picture of these to send to Miley," she said. The pancakes smelled even better than they looked, which was really saying something. A couple of the strawberries had been cut so they fanned out and formed little rose-shaped garnishes. JoJo snapped a picture of her beautiful breakfast and quickly sent it off to her BFF with some heart emojis. Miley was in school, so JoJo knew she wouldn't be able to reply to the text for a while, but she also knew Miley would be happy to have a text waiting for her. Unable to wait even one more second, JoJo took an enormous bite.

"Well, are they as good as they look?" her mom asked while JoJo chewed.

JoJo nodded and widened her eyes to show her appreciation. "They. Are. Amazing," she said once she finally swallowed. "Give me your plate."

"Only if you'll take a piece of this French toast," her mom said, cutting off a generous wedge. "Today we're celebrating."

"Deal." JoJo giggled, trading her mom a wedge of her pancakes for the syrupy French toast. "I'm going to need all the energy I can get!"

A few hours later, JoJo was relaxing with BowBow in her pink-and-teal bedroom.

"BowBow, any last words of wisdom before I leave for class?" JoJo asked.

It was almost time to leave for dance class. The morning had seemed to crawl by after breakfast. JoJo had completed all of her homeschool assignments for the day, then changed into her favorite sparkly dancing gear for class. After debating for quite a while about which bow gave her the perfect "first day of dance workshop" look, JoJo had finally settled on a black one with clear rhinestones. It was one of her favorites, and it looked really cute with her black leggings and hot pink sequined top.

"Um, excuse me, BowBow! I asked you a question."

As if on cue, BowBow barked.

"That's excellent advice!" JoJo cried, scooping up her little dog and giving her a kiss on the head. "I will definitely make sure to have *the best* time!"

JoJo placed BowBow back on the ground and took one last look around her room to make sure she had everything she needed. She triple-checked her backpack for her lucky water bottle and her favorite hair ties. She was pretty sure she had everything. She caught a glimpse of herself in the mirror over her dresser and smiled. "Let's do this," she told her reflection. She looked sparkly. She looked good. She looked like a dancer who was ready for anything.

CHAPTER 2

"JoJo Siwa, welcome to my studio."

A petite woman with short black hair greeted JoJo, a clipboard tucked under one arm, her other arm extended to shake hands. "I'm Roberta Robbins. I will be your instructor."

JoJo knew exactly who Roberta Robbins was—she was one of the best choreographers on the planet! She'd been a dancing legend on Broadway for years before

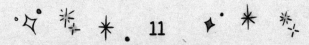

becoming a choreographer for some of the most famous dancers in the business. Roberta's soft, husky voice was even familiar to JoJo because she'd watched videos on YouTube of Roberta being interviewed. Roberta had been at JoJo's audition but had not said a word; she'd simply nodded when JoJo finished her routine.

"It's nice to meet you," JoJo replied, shaking Roberta's hand. "I'm so excited to be here! Thank you for offering me a spot. I can't wait for class to begin!"

"Good," Roberta replied, nodding briskly. "I like your energy—I remember that about you from your audition. Now go inside and meet the other girls. Class will begin in a little while, after everyone has arrived and gotten settled."

Murmuring her thanks, JoJo walked past Roberta, took a deep breath, and looked around. The studio looked very similar to the dozens of others JoJo had danced in. The central room was large and airy, with floor-to-ceiling mirrors running along the front wall. The side walls were painted light peach, and the wooden floors had that perfectly scuffed look that JoJo associated with dance studios. JoJo smiled, thinking of all the pairs of feet that had danced on these very floors under Roberta's expert guidance. A long, wooden ballet barre was attached to the mirrors, and an additional barre was attached to one of the side walls.

"Pretty cool being here, right?" A girl who looked to be about sixteen had walked up next to JoJo. JoJo turned to greet her, but the girl continued talking. "I'm Belle. *Belle Manning?*"

From the way she said her name, JoJo had the feeling she was supposed to know who

Belle was, but the girl didn't look familiar to her. She was tall and slim, her light brown hair wrapped up in a bun on top of her head. JoJo was sure she'd never met her. "I'm JoJo," she began. But again, the girl kept talking.

"I *know* who you are!" Belle exclaimed, her pretty hazel eyes lighting up as she smiled. "I'm a fan! It's so cool you're in this class! I thought you might know who I am too. I mean, I'm not as famous as you, but I've had a few spots in some professional videos— probably people you know from Nickelodeon award shows and stuff..." Belle's voice trailed off as she looked at JoJo expectantly.

"It's nice to meet you," JoJo said with a smile. She definitely didn't know Belle, but she didn't want to say that. "It *is* really cool being here," JoJo added, answering Belle's initial question. "I've been counting down the days until the workshop begins! Literally marking them off on my calendar!"

"That's cute," Belle replied. JoJo noticed she'd wrinkled her nose a little when she said it. "I want you to meet someone," she said, taking JoJo's arm and pulling her across the room to where a dancer was stretching at the barre along the wall. "This is Bahi. We just met, but she's the best. We should all be friends. Bahi, this is JoJo Siwa!"

Once again, the way Belle spoke left JoJo with the impression that there was a deeper meaning to what she'd said. In this case, she was pretty sure Belle and Bahi must have spotted her when she walked in and had been trying to decide who she was.

Bahi looked up from her deep stretch and smiled. She looked to be about Belle's age and was beautiful, with warm brown skin and shiny black hair worn in a bun, just like Belle's. "It's nice to meet you, JoJo. I'm a big fan! I absolutely loved your performance at the Kids' Choice Awards, and—"

"Don't gush," Belle said sharply, cutting Bahi off. She looked at JoJo and rolled her eyes. *Sorry*, she mouthed.

"That's okay!" JoJo replied, smiling warmly at Bahi. She'd noticed the way the smile had fallen from Bahi's face when Belle snapped at her, and JoJo felt for the other girl. "Hearing someone is a fan never gets old," she continued. "Thank you so much! I'm excited to be in class with you! So, where are you—"

JoJo was just about to ask Bahi where she lived and what kind of dance she specialized in, but once again Belle spoke over her. "So the break room is back there," she told JoJo, pointing to a door off the back wall of the studio. "Everyone gets their own cubby for

16

your stuff. You can write your name on your cubby. Pick one close to mine!"

"Thanks." JoJo appreciated that Belle was trying to show her the ropes, but there was something about her that made JoJo feel a little uneasy. She definitely didn't care for the way Belle had snapped at Bahi. However, JoJo believed in giving everyone a chance. Some people just didn't make great first impressions. And some people started off on the wrong foot and then changed for the better and turned into great friends. JoJo thought of her friend Kyra, whom she and her closest friends had met over the summer. When they'd first met Kyra, she wasn't very nice to their friend Grace, because she was jealous of her. But Kyra had apologized to Grace, and now the two girls were practically BFFs.

"I just realized, I'm still wearing my jacket!" JoJo laughed and shrugged her backpack off her shoulder. "I'm gonna go drop my stuff off and—"

"And you can fix your hair when you're back there," Belle finished.

"What?" JoJo asked, unsure if she had heard Belle correctly.

"You can fix your hair when you're back there," Belle repeated. "You're not planning to wear it in a side pony with that rhinestone bow during class, are you?"

"Belle, that's her signature look," Bahi whispered, just loudly enough for JoJo to hear.

"I know *that*," Belle replied, rolling her eyes at Bahi. Then she turned her gaze back to JoJo. "I just think that hairdo isn't very . . . *appropriate* for class. You should put your hair up in a bun like Bahi and I did."

"Thanks, I'm good." JoJo was sure now that her gut had been right about Belle. She probably wasn't going to end up close friends with her. But that was okay. As much as JoJo loved making new friends, she knew not everyone was meant to become a friend. And first and foremost, she was there to dance! "I'm going to go get settled in. See you in a bit," she added, waving as she walked away.

JoJo made her way to the break room and found it already occupied by a handful of other girls. The girls appeared to be older teens and stood together chatting and laughing. From their simple pale pink and black leotards and flowy skirts, JoJo was sure they were ballerinas. It seemed as if they all knew each other—the professional ballet community was a small one, after all. The girls smiled at JoJo as she claimed a cubby and began removing her jacket. JoJo smiled back.

Just then, a petite but powerful-looking girl dressed in a blue tracksuit walked into the room, and suddenly, everyone stopped talking and stared. Then, realizing it, the ballerinas laughed nervously and waved to the girl before resuming their chatter.

Now, this girl *was* someone JoJo recognized. She was Michelle Lee, the famous ice dancer! Miley was a huge fan of Michelle's, and JoJo was a pretty big fan too. She'd seen Michelle skate on television in major competitions many times and had always admired the grace and skill Michelle brought to her sport. At just sixteen years old, she was one of the youngest and most accomplished ice dancers in the country. JoJo couldn't believe the famous athlete was in this workshop. She couldn't wait to tell Miley!

Michelle settled at a cubby near JoJo's, scribbled her initials on the wipe-off board in front, peeled off her jacket to reveal a colorful bodysuit, and began placing her personal items in the bin.

"Hi, Michelle, I'm JoJo Siwa." JoJo gave Michelle a little wave a few moments later. "I'm a big fan of yours. Congrats on winning silver in last year's games!"

"Thanks," Michelle replied. She turned to face JoJo as she began pulling her shiny dark hair into a ponytail. A look of recognition crossed her face. "Wait, I know who you are! You're a singer, right? I've seen you on Nickelodeon . . ."

"Yep, that's me." JoJo held up a hand. "Guilty!"

Michelle nodded and gave JoJo a quick smile. "Nice meeting you. I'll see you out there!"

"Sounds good," JoJo called as Michelle walked away. JoJo finished stowing her belongings in her bin and wrote her name, big and bold, across the wipe-off board.

As she headed back into the studio, JoJo saw Michelle across the room near the wall barre. She seemed to be walking away from Belle and Bahi, who had another girl with them. JoJo noticed that Michelle was frowning. Belle spotted JoJo and waved her over. JoJo sighed quietly. She really didn't want to spend more time with Belle before class began, but she also didn't want to be rude. She made her way over to the group.

"JoJo, this is Gabrielle—but we're calling her Bree," Belle said, pointing to a petite girl who was busily fixing her blond hair into a bun. "Bree, this is JoJo Siwa. She's a *cool* famous person—unlike Michelle Lee."

Before JoJo could say anything, Belle continued. "We just tried introducing ourselves to Michelle Lee, and she was so unfriendly," Belle whispered to JoJo. "Right, guys?"

Bree shrugged uncomfortably, bobby pins sticking out of her mouth as she tried to fix her hair, which didn't seem to want to stay put, while Bahi shook her head. "I don't think she was being unfriendly. I think maybe she's just shy."

"Yeah, I met her in the break room, and she seemed nice," JoJo added.

"Whatever." Belle rolled her eyes. "Anyway, JoJo, do you have any sort of a B nickname you can go by? Any chance your middle name begins with a B and we can call you that?"

"Wait, what?" JoJo couldn't help but laugh. Had Belle really just asked her to change her name? "Oh, wait, you're not joking?"

"Of course I'm not joking," Belle said seriously. "Bahi, Bree, and I are calling ourselves the Queen Bs. We plan to be the queens of this workshop. We like you, so you can be part of our group . . . if you can think of a *B* name to use."

"Thanks, I'm good," JoJo said. She realized that this was the second time she'd said that to Belle since meeting her. She could tell her response annoyed Belle, but she didn't let it bother her. She thought of a saying her dad had taught her: *You can satisfy some of the people some of the time, but you can't satisfy all the people all the time.*

JoJo was glad when Roberta made her way up to the front of the room. Everyone fell silent, waiting to hear what she would say. There was something about Roberta that just commanded attention.

"Welcome, girls. Gather around," she said softly, spreading out her arms. The dancers gravitated toward the center of the floor, in front of Roberta. "I am happy to have you all here with me," Roberta began, her blue eyes scanning every face in the room as she spoke. "You have all worked hard and accomplished great things so far in your careers. You're here because you are gifted."

"That's right! Gifted!" Belle said loudly, snapping her fingers. She giggled nervously when no one else said anything. Roberta fixed Belle with an even stare, and JoJo noticed that Belle blushed and looked at the ground. She was pretty sure that was the last time Belle would interrupt their instructor!

"As I was saying, you are all gifted—but you are here to *work*. This class will not be easy, and it might not always be fun, but I am here to give you tools to become even better dancers. What I ask of *you* is that you work hard, respect each other, and—most of all—respect yourselves."

Once again, Roberta scanned the faces of the dancers in the room, making eye contact with every girl. When her eyes met JoJo's, JoJo nodded ever so slightly. She wanted Roberta to know she had her respect and that she was there to work hard and to learn.

JoJo felt a chill travel up her spine. She'd never had a dance instructor who was as serious, and as intimidating, as Roberta. But JoJo was ready for it. She stood up even straighter, ready to face every challenge this workshop had to offer.

CHAPTER 3

"Tell me again exactly what Michelle Lee said when you met her," Miley was saying between mouthfuls of pizza. "Wait, no, tell me exactly what she's been wearing every time you've seen her. Oh, and does she wear nail polish? Tell me she loves glitter as much as I do!"

JoJo laughed and tossed her wadded-up napkin at her best friend. Miley was even more excited that Michelle Lee was in JoJo's

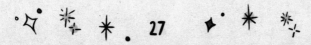

workshop than JoJo had expected her to be. It was Friday night, and Miley was sleeping over at JoJo's. They'd already eaten dinner a few hours earlier but had gotten hungry again and were polishing off some leftover pizza.

"I told you, I haven't really gotten to talk to her that much," JoJo replied, pulling a piece of pepperoni off her slice and popping it into her mouth. "I met her the first day, and she was friendly, but since then she mostly keeps to herself. During breaks she just drinks water and checks her phone. She seems really serious...driven—you know what I mean? She's not super bubbly or anything like that, but she's nice. She's there to work. We all are."

"Well, except for that girl, Belle," Miley said, grimacing. She flicked a section of her long, light brown curls over one shoulder. "It sounds like she's just there to boss people around and make them change their names and hairstyles!"

JoJo had already completed three days of classes and had told Miley all about her experiences, including details about the other dancers in the workshop. And how sore she was from the intense workout she was getting!

"The thing about Belle is that she's actually an incredible dancer," JoJo said thoughtfully. "She's really talented—everyone in the workshop is. Each dancer has her own strengths," JoJo explained. "The ballerinas are all so graceful—and you wouldn't believe how strong they are! Bahi, one of the Queen Bs, picks up everything really fast—I feel like she's a choreographer's dream! And Bree, the other Queen B, has a ton of raw talent, but she's probably struggling the most out of everyone in class. She definitely has the skills, but she seems to lack confidence. When she gets nervous, she messes up."

"Well, it sounds like her buddy Belle isn't helping her in that department," Miley commented.

JoJo nodded. She'd told Miley about how whenever Bree made a little mistake in class, Belle was always quick to comment on it. She also told Miley how Belle had claimed she did it to help Bree, but JoJo didn't see how being picked on by your supposed friend was helpful. "I hope I'm wrong about Belle, or that she loosens up from here on out. Maybe she just had first-week jitters and will calm down next week."

"I hope so," Miley said, reaching over to steal a piece of crust from JoJo's plate. "But I have a bad feeling she's not going to change. Anyway! Moving on to more pleasant topics:

Tell me more about this performance that's happening! And the solo that I just know you are going to nab!"

"Oh, right, the performance and the solo!" JoJo got so excited, she sprang from her chair and began spontaneously dancing around the kitchen. BowBow, who had been napping at her feet, jumped up and yipped excitedly.

"We get all the details next week, but we will be putting on a performance at the arts center on Valentine's Day. Roberta announced at the end of class today that one student from the workshop will be chosen to perform a solo. I really want to get it, Miley!" JoJo's eyes were shining as she stopped moving for a moment and stood totally still. "I will have to work harder than I've ever worked before, but I think I have a shot at the solo, and I would looooove to get it!"

"You will totally get it!" Miley cheered, leaping up from the table to hug JoJo. Miley was a big hugger. "You're one of the best dancers I've ever seen. And no one puts more into a performance than you do! You would be the perfect choice for it!"

"Aww, thanks, Miley." JoJo grinned, returning the hug. Miley was a fantastic choreographer in her own right, so the fact that she believed so strongly in JoJo's talent meant a lot. Miley also knew firsthand how hard JoJo worked and that, when she set her mind to something, she could be *super* determined.

As Miley sat back down, JoJo picked up BowBow and shimmied around the table with the little pup in her arms. "Since the performance is on Valentine's Day, I keep wondering if it will be V-Day themed," JoJo mused aloud. "It's torture not knowing all the details! In fact, I think Roberta told us at the end of class just to torment us, knowing we wouldn't be able to think about anything else all weekend!"

"You might be right about that," Miley agreed. "We choreographers like getting into the heads of our dancers!" She waggled her eyebrows, and JoJo giggled. "But no matter what happens, I'll be there cheering for you! And I bet Jacob, Grace, and Kyra will want to go too. Oh, that reminds me . . ." Miley snapped her fingers. "I promised Grace and Kyra we'd call them both tonight so we can figure out plans for our Valentine's sleepover."

Miley and JoJo had been friends with Jacob forever, but Grace and Kyra were newer friends. Miley, Jacob, Grace, and Kyra all went to school together, but all five of them hung out together every chance they got.

Just then, JoJo's brother, Jayden, walked into the kitchen. "Did you guys leave any pizza for me?"

"Nope. We ate it all. The *entire* extra-pepperoni pie Mom ordered," JoJo said. She put down BowBow and dramatically rubbed her stomach and groaned. "And uuuuhhhh . . . I think I overdid it just a bit!" She put a hand over her mouth and pre-tended to dash for the bathroom.

"What?" Jayden's eyes got huge, and Miley burst out laughing.

"I'm kidding!" JoJo giggled. "There are six slices left in there." She pointed to the refrig-erator. "Knock yourself out."

With that, JoJo and Miley cleared off the table. JoJo quickly rinsed their plates and popped them into the dishwasher. Then she peered over her brother's shoulder into the refrigerator.

"Did you have enough, Miley? Should we bring a few more slices up to my room to eat while we call Grace and Kyra?"

"I think I'm good for now," Miley said. "We can always come back later for a midnight snack!"

A little while later the girls were seated on JoJo's bed, surrounded by pillows, Bow-Bow snoozing between them. JoJo's phone began playing "Boomerang"—her ringtone for Grace—and JoJo quickly answered the call and put it on speaker.

"Hey!" Kyra's and Grace's voices rang out through the speaker.

"Are you guys together?" JoJo asked.

"Yeah, we're having a sleepover at my house," Grace replied.

JoJo could imagine Grace smiling shyly on the other end of the phone. She was glad that Grace and Kyra had grown so close. JoJo thought about how, just a few months ago, it had seemed that maybe Grace and Kyra would never be friends, let alone close friends who had sleepovers. JoJo hoped that she was wrong about Belle too.

"Earth to JoJo," Miley was saying, snapping her fingers in front of JoJo's face.

JoJo blinked and laughed. "Sorry, I zoned out for a second there. It's not you—I love you guys—I'm just exhausted from my dance workshop."

"That's right!" Kyra exclaimed on the other end of the phone, the excitement in her voice clear. "Tell us all about it!"

JoJo quickly brought her friends up to speed on everything about her first week of class, including the fact that Michelle Lee was one of her classmates.

"Do you think you could ask her for her autograph for me?" Grace asked.

"I'm already a step ahead of you," Miley said before JoJo could reply. "I'm convincing JoJo to make plans to hang out with her after class sometime, and then we can all meet her!"

"Hey, wait a second," JoJo said, holding up a hand. "I don't remember agreeing to that! I told you, I've barely spoken to her, and—"

"I know," Miley said, her dark eyes twinkling. "But it'll happen eventually. How can she not love you and want to hang out and meet your fabulous besties?"

JoJo laughed along with the other girls at Miley's silliness. JoJo knew that as much as Miley would really love to meet Michelle Lee, she would never, ever expect JoJo to try to make it happen unless it came up naturally.

Eventually the girls switched topics and began planning their Valentine's Day sleepover. The sleepover was an annual tradition for JoJo and Miley, and this year they had decided to include Grace and Kyra, since they were quickly becoming a foursome. As the girls ran through the dates that they were free, they realized they would have to have the sleepover a couple of weeks early, because JoJo would be going out of town the weekend after Valentine's Day, and Grace was going to visit her sister at college the weekend before.

"So February second it is," JoJo said, drawing a heart around the date in red marker on her calendar. "That's next weekend! It will be here before we know it!"

"Can I bring anything?" Kyra asked. "Snacks? Candy?"

Whenever the group hung out at Kyra's house, she was always the ultimate hostess, making sure that everyone had just the right snacks at all times. She never forgot to have plenty of braces-friendly treats on hand for Jacob and Grace. JoJo loved how thoughtful she was.

"Oh, we'll have plenty of candy from the—" JoJo clamped a hand over her mouth to prevent herself from saying more. She'd had a super fun idea for a surprise she was making for her friends to give them at the sleepover. But she didn't want to spoil the surprise and tell them about it yet.

"What was that?" Miley asked, giving JoJo a suspicious look.

"It's a surprise," JoJo said, giggling at the look on Miley's face. "You'll just have to wait and see!

CHAPTER 4

JoJo dropped her backpack into her cubby in the break room and sat down to change into her dancing slippers. It was Monday afternoon, and the first class since Roberta had announced the solo was about to begin.

"Darn it, I forgot a hair tie," Michelle Lee muttered from her neighboring cubby.

"Oh, I got you!" JoJo said, reaching into her backpack. She always kept an extra stash of hair ties in her bag, just in case. She held out an assortment of glittery hair ties to Michelle.

"Thanks," Michelle said gratefully, grabbing a blue one and pulling her hair back into a quick ponytail.

"Anytime. I also have a huge stash of bows if you ever want one," JoJo added, gesturing to the tie-dyed bow she wore in her own hair.

"I do love your bows! I might take you up on that for one of my skating performances," Michelle said, a huge grin spreading over her face. "Maybe it will bring me good luck!"

JoJo grinned back and waved as Michelle left the break room.

"Oh, so are you guys best friends now?"

JoJo hadn't heard Belle come into the room, but there she was. She took a deep breath and tried to keep her voice even. "Oh, hi, Belle. I'll see you out there," JoJo said, getting up and walking out of the room. There was no point in responding to Belle's snarky question, so JoJo chose to ignore it.

JoJo walked into the main room, spotted the ballerinas warming up at the barre along the wall, and made her way toward them. The older girls were all very friendly, but JoJo's favorite was Jamilla. Jamilla had an extra warm smile for JoJo when she saw her and moved over to make room for her at the barre.

"How's it going?" Jamilla asked her as she raised an arm above her head and arched back, gently stretching out her spine. Her movements were so graceful that she reminded JoJo of a cat.

"Good! Though I think I woke up feeling even sorer today, if that's humanly possible." JoJo grimaced as she began stretching her own back.

"Did you remember to stretch a lot over the weekend?" Jamilla asked, a frown clouding her pretty features. "You have to make sure to stretch a lot to keep limber between classes."

"Oh, yeah, I know." JoJo nodded. "I thought I stretched enough, but maybe not. Thanks for the tip!"

"Anytime." Jamilla winked. "I think it's so great that you're in this class, keeping up with all of us older girls. Even dancing circles around some of us! You're pretty amazing—you know that?"

JoJo blushed. Jamilla was a professional ballerina and one of the most graceful dancers JoJo had ever seen, and she was telling her *she* was amazing. That made JoJo *feel* amazing. "That means a lot, coming from you," she said sincerely. "You are just— wow. You are *so* graceful! You even walk beautifully. In fact, you don't walk—you *glide!*"

"I'll take that compliment!" Jamilla beamed.

Just then, Roberta made her way to the front of the classroom, and a hush fell over the group. Class was about to begin.

"All right, girls, as I mentioned on Friday, one of you will be chosen at the end of the workshop to perform the solo during our show on Valentine's Day. Each of you will learn the routine, which I will share with you in a moment, and then on the last day of the workshop, the dancer who performs the routine the best will be chosen for the solo. Are there any questions?"

Bahi raised her hand to ask about costumes for the performance, and Roberta explained that in honor of Valentine's Day, their costumes would be red. Red leotards with glittery trim around the neckline, and flowy red skirts.

"Do we have to wear our hair in buns?" Bree asked, earning a scowl from Belle.

"No, you can wear your hair however you choose, as long as the audience can see your face," Roberta replied.

JoJo thought about all the red bows she had in her closet at home and wondered which one would look the best with her costume. She bounced up and down on her toes, feeling adrenaline pumping through her body. She couldn't wait to learn the routine!

"I will be breaking you into two groups to practice together . . ."

JoJo crossed her fingers that she wouldn't get put into a group with Belle, but no such luck. As Roberta announced the groups,

JoJo found herself with the Queen Bs and Michelle. The ballerinas were in their own group.

Roberta performed the routine in its entirety twice for the group. The girls burst into applause each time after she finished. The routine was fantastic—it was *beyond* fantastic! JoJo had never seen a dance that was so complex, graceful, and beautiful all at the same time. She couldn't wait to learn it!

As the girls broke off into their groups to begin learning the first part of the routine, Roberta recommended that they eventually settle into smaller groups of two and three. Michelle appeared at JoJo's side. "Wanna be my partner?" she asked.

"Yes, please!" JoJo grinned. She knew the Queen Bs would be sticking together, and it felt nice to have Michelle ask her to partner up.

JoJo and Michelle quickly fell into an easy rhythm. JoJo marveled at how Michelle never seemed to get tired, no matter how many times they ran through a particularly grueling part of the routine.

"You're a superhuman! You're in ridiculous shape," JoJo told Michelle a little while later when they paused to catch their breath.

"You're no slouch in that department yourself," Michelle said, grinning as she took a swig of water. She tightened her ponytail and nodded. "Plus, you've already pretty much nailed the whole beginning of the routine, even that really hard part that everyone is struggling with. I think you've got a real shot at getting the solo."

"Thanks. I'm used to having to learn new routines really quickly for my performances. But I've clearly got some stiff competition." JoJo gestured to the other dancers around the room. "I think every girl here has a shot at the solo."

"Agreed." Michelle nodded and put down her water bottle. "OK, ready to take it from the—"

"Seriously, Bree, do you have two left feet? Why is it taking you so long to pick this up?"

Belle's voice rang out loud and clear, because she was shouting. JoJo looked over to where the Queen Bs were huddled. She hadn't been paying much attention to how the routine was going for them—she was too focused on working with Michelle—but from the look of it, things weren't going well. Belle's face was bright red, and her hands were on her hips as she towered over Bree, who was sprawled on the floor. Bree looked ready to burst into tears. And Bahi, who was usually perfectly pulled together, looked so frazzled that a few strands of hair fell from her normally flawless bun.

Michelle caught JoJo's eye and said quietly, "Let Roberta deal with it. Don't let her distract you."

JoJo nodded but kept an eye on the Queen Bs for another moment until Roberta rushed over to Bree. JoJo knew she couldn't afford to get distracted, but somebody needed to make sure Bree was okay.

JoJo and Michelle walked to a vacant corner on the other side of the room to give Roberta privacy while she talked to the Queen Bs.

"She's such a bully," Michelle said quietly, nodding her head in Belle's direction. "She is why I usually keep to myself. I mean, I get it, we're all competitors here, but some people just take it way too far. I've had to deal with my fair share of bullies coming up in my

49

sport, and it's just *exhausting*. No one needs that drama."

JoJo nodded. Like Michelle, she'd also dealt with her fair share of bullies and knew how terrible it felt if you let them get under your skin.

"Wait, what I am saying?" Michelle said suddenly. "You know about this sort of stuff! My cousin Amanda is a *huge* fan of yours, and she was telling me all about the Siwanatorz and how your fans all stand up for each other and are totally against bullying."

JoJo grinned the way she always did when she was reminded of the Siwanatorz and how proud they made her. "That is so nice to hear," JoJo said earnestly. "I'd love to meet your cousin if she ever wants to meet me."

"The next time she's out here visiting me, I will definitely take you up on that offer," Michelle replied. "She was basically freaking out when I told her you were one of the dancers in this workshop! I can't tell you how excited she would be! Are you sure wouldn't mind?"

"I love meeting my fans," JoJo assured her. "Besides, my best friends are kind of dying to meet you, so let's exchange numbers later, and we can set something up!"

Michelle nodded. "Sounds perfect! I'd love to meet your friends! And before we get back to work . . ." Michelle looked down at the ground shyly and cleared her throat. "I'm glad you're here. I meant what I said before about how I usually keep to myself in competitive situations because, well, I've had to deal with people in skating who will do anything to win, and I've had some pretty bad experiences. But I feel like we can compete against each other for the solo and still be friends."

"We can!" JoJo touched Michelle's arm. "I'm sorry you've had to deal with that. Winning is important, but it's not *everything*, and no one can win all the time. Nothing is more important than treating other people with respect. Even Roberta said so."

Michelle nodded. "Speaking of Roberta . . . let's get back to work!"

A short while later, JoJo and Michelle rejoined the Queen Bs. All five girls had learned the first part of the routine, and it was time for each of them to perform it for the rest of her group and receive feedback.

Michelle went first and sailed through the routine almost perfectly. She struggled a little bit with the one tricky combination that JoJo knew everyone was having a hard time with, but she had improved tremendously in just a couple of hours.

"Great job!" JoJo cheered. "You've almost got that tough part down! You'll have it in no time!"

"Thanks to your help," Michelle said, taking a swig of water.

"That part is giving me trouble too," Bree said uncertainly. "JoJo, would you mind working with me for a few minutes? Maybe you can help me."

"Sure," JoJo replied. "Let's go over there and—"

"Bree, I already helped you with that for twenty minutes!" Belle interjected loudly, cutting JoJo off. "If you don't know it by now, you should just give up, because you're *never* going to get it!"

The other four girls in the group fell silent for a moment, and then JoJo spoke up, making sure to keep her tone light. "Hey, Belle, I'm pretty sure that's not what Roberta had in mind when she said to treat each other with respect."

As Belle registered that JoJo had just spoken up to her, her face clouded over, and JoJo had the impression Belle was about to erupt. But then her expression changed, and she walked over to Bree and put a hand on her shoulder in a friendly way. "You know what would be great, JoJo?" she said in a super sweet voice that sounded nothing like the harsh tone she'd been using moments earlier. "If you could maybe help Bree with that one really hard part. I think she's *almost* got it. Can you do that?"

It took JoJo a moment to figure out what Belle's game was, but then she noticed Roberta. JoJo wasn't sure when the instructor had arrived at their side of the room or how much she had witnessed, but she was there now and watching Belle very closely.

"How is it going over here, girls?" Roberta asked, her eyes on Belle.

"Great!" A smile lit up Belle's face. "Bree was struggling just a little bit with one part—we're all having a hard time with it, but Bree especially—so I was just asking JoJo if maybe she could help her with it, since she seems to have picked it up already."

Roberta nodded, her expression unreadable. "Yes, JoJo, please work with Bree for a bit, if you don't mind."

"I don't mind at all," JoJo said.

As JoJo walked away with Bree, she could feel Belle's angry eyes following her. She knew she had made Belle mad, and while she didn't want to deal with Belle's drama, she knew that standing up to her had been the right thing to do.

CHAPTER 5

Two hours later, JoJo was settling into her mom's car to go home after class.

"So, how was it?" Jessalyn asked as JoJo buckled her seat belt.

"We started learning the solo today," JoJo replied. "Mom, wait until you see this number Roberta choreographed. It's out of this world! We spent the whole class today learning just the beginning part. It's probably the most challenging routine I've ever learned, but it'll be so worth it! There's one combination that's giving everyone a little trouble, but I think I've almost got it. I can do it right *most* of the time."

JoJo's mom kept her eyes on the road but nodded and smiled as she listened. "Maybe you can show it to me at home. If I know you, you'll be practicing nonstop between now and audition day for the solo."

"Of course," JoJo agreed, already tumbling into her next thought. "Everyone in the class is so good—it would be a major accomplishment to land the solo." JoJo stopped talking for a moment and looked out the window. "There was actually a little drama in class today with some of the other dancers. Drama that sort of involved me . . ."

Jessalyn shot JoJo a concerned look. "What's going on?"

JoJo explained to her mom about Belle's behavior and how she'd been bullying

Gabrielle. "Bree asked me to help her with this part of the routine that I was having an easier time with, so I did. But Belle tried to say that Bree should just give up, so I reminded her that Roberta had asked us all to be respectful of one another, and Belle sort of turned her drama on me."

"How so?"

"Well, before that happened, everything was going pretty great. I was partnered with Michelle Lee for the first half of class, and we were getting along really well. It turns out her cousin is a Siwanator, so we talked about that, and I told her I'd love to meet her cousin. And we talked about maybe hanging out sometime so she can meet my friends."

"I'm sure Miley would like that." Jessalyn smiled.

"Exactly," JoJo continued. "Grace and Kyra too! Anyway, Michelle and I were a great team, and then all the drama happened with Belle. I went off to help Bree, and then we all took a break, and after that everything just felt different." JoJo paused. "Mom, what are we doing?"

Jessalyn had turned the car into a strip mall a few miles away from their house. She parked the car in an open spot and turned to face JoJo. "I wanted to be able to give you my full attention," Jessalyn explained. "Also, it sounds like you might need ice cream," she added, pointing to a shop called Cups and Cones.

JoJo grinned. Her mom was, hands down, the *best*. She always knew just what JoJo needed.

"Ice cream is *exactly* what I need!" Her mom smiled and nodded for JoJo to continue with her story. "You know that feeling you get when you walk into a room and you're pretty sure everyone was just talking about you?"

"I think I know what you mean."

"Well, after I helped Bree and we took our break, I went to get my phone so I could exchange numbers with Michelle. When I walked into the kitchen area, everyone went silent. The Queen Bs, but also Michelle. I thought maybe I was imagining it, but then one of the ballerinas, this girl named Lindsay, said something to me about how the ballerinas all know they probably won't get the solo, so I should know that none of them is trying to take it from me."

"Wait, what?" Jessalyn frowned. "You didn't get the solo already, did you?"

"No, of course not!" JoJo threw her hands up in exasperation. "We all just started learning it! But apparently Belle told everyone that I think the solo is already mine because I'm famous or whatever and that I was complaining that the other girls were trying to steal it from me. My friend Jamilla told me Belle was spreading it all around just as I walked in for my phone. Luckily, Jamilla shrugged it off—she's super chill—but can you believe it?"

"Honey, anyone who knows you knows you're not like that." Jessalyn reached over to give JoJo a supportive squeeze on the knee. "I know it's hard, but you have to just rise above it all."

"You're right," JoJo agreed. "But it felt like the whole dynamic in class was weird after that. Between Belle being a bully and then acting super sweet when Roberta was watching, and some of the girls maybe believing that I think I'm entitled to the solo, there's so *much* drama! The dancing is intense enough without it." JoJo took a deep breath and shook her head as if to clear her thoughts. "I know I can't worry about what other people think," she said finally. "And I'm not going to let Belle ruin this for me!"

Jessalyn gave JoJo a one-armed hug over the console. "I'm proud of you, honey. And you're right. You earned this opportunity. Make the most of it."

"Thanks, Mom." JoJo felt a million times better, the way she always did after she talked to her mom. "Now I think you mentioned something about ice cream . . . ?"

That evening, JoJo went to work putting the finishing touches on her special Valentine's Day surprises for Miley, Grace, and Kyra. She had all her supplies spread out around her on the kitchen table and was so focused on writing Miley's name in glitter on a plastic bag that she almost didn't notice when her brother sat down at the table.

"Nice candy stash." Jayden nodded approvingly at the piles of candy JoJo had carefully laid out. He reached out to grab a piece from Grace's pile, and JoJo swatted his hand away.

"The candy in these piles is off-limits!" she said. "It's for my Candy Kisses for Valentine's Day. I've already counted out the perfect number of pieces for all my friends, so no touching!"

Jayden looked so disappointed that JoJo couldn't help but laugh. "There's extra in the pantry that you can help yourself to. But don't eat it all . . . I might need some for later!"

"Thank you!" Jayden said excitedly. "What's a Candy Kiss? Is that like a candygram?"

"It's a candygram with a little something extra," JoJo explained, putting the cap on the blue glitter pen she'd been using. "My personal twist is that each bag of candy comes with a note from me, saying why I love that friend so much."

"And all the glitter and stickers and stuff?" Jayden gestured to the art supplies JoJo had all over the table.

"To decorate the bags," JoJo replied. "I'm personalizing each one. Glitter for Miley, unicorns for Grace, and hearts and lots of bright pink for Kyra, since that's her favorite color."

"That's really cool." Jayden nodded. "You can keep mine simple, by the way. You can just write *best brother ever* and leave it at that. No glitter for me."

"You wish." JoJo laughed and threw a chocolate-covered caramel from Miley's pile at Jayden.

"I get to keep this one now!" he said, popping the chocolate into his mouth and running away before JoJo could stop him.

An hour or so later, JoJo's Candy Kisses were complete. It had felt great to put down on paper why each of her friends was so special to her. It was the perfect antidote to all the drama that had happened at dance class that day.

JoJo couldn't wait for the weekend, for their sleepover, to give the Candy Kisses to her BFFs!

CHAPTER 6

JoJo practiced hard on Tuesday evening after a long day of studying and managed to master the one part of the routine that had been giving everyone a little bit of trouble. When she got to the dance studio on Wednesday, the first thing she noticed was that Roberta had put up Valentine's Day decorations. Red-and-white paper hearts adorned the walls of the studio, and a chubby cardboard cutout cupid was hanging

in the kitchen, surrounded by pink streamers. There were even heart decals at the top
of the mirrored wall! JoJo knew it must have
been a lot of work for Roberta to decorate
the studio. She smiled, thinking that even
though Roberta had a pretty tough exterior,
she clearly loved Valentine's Day as much as
JoJo did!

JoJo and the other dancers gathered in the
center of the room as class began. Roberta
explained that she wanted each dancer to
perform the first section of the routine so she
could see their progress. JoJo was extra glad
she'd put in all that time practicing.

As the dancers took turns performing
under Roberta's watchful gaze, JoJo could see
that most of them had improved a lot. Some
still struggled a little bit to master the trick-
iest combination, but overall everyone was
doing well.

She crossed her fingers for Bree when it was her turn.

"Break a leg," Belle called, smirking, as Bree took her place in the center of the room.

JoJo noticed the way Bree stiffened at the sound of Belle's voice and hoped Belle's comment didn't throw her off.

Bree took her place and began dancing. Within moments, she seemed to get lost in the routine and danced beautifully. She made a couple of small missteps during the toughest part, but she recovered well. JoJo could tell Bree had been practicing a lot. As Bree finished and took a bow, she caught JoJo's eye. JoJo grinned and gave her a thumbs-up. From the way she smiled and walked confidently back to the Queen Bs, JoJo could see that Bree felt really good about her performance, and she was glad—Bree deserved to feel good about what she had done!

"Too bad you messed up that one exchange in the middle," Belle said loudly as Bree rejoined the Queen Bs. "You just can't seem to figure that part out, can you?"

JoJo watched in horror as Bree's shoulders slumped, all the confidence she'd felt a minute ago appearing to drain away.

"No commentary from the other dancers," Roberta said firmly from the front of the room, looking over in the direction of the Queen Bs.

"Oh, I was just telling Bree how great she did!" Belle replied, smiling sweetly.

"As I said, no commentary from the dancers," Roberta repeated. "JoJo, you're up."

JoJo walked to the center of the room and took a deep breath, clearing her mind. She wasn't going to think about Belle or Bree or even Roberta. She was just going to do what she loved—*dance*.

The music started, and JoJo began moving. Before she knew it, the routine was over, and she bowed. She knew she'd done well; she could feel it. She looked up from her bow and waited for Roberta's reaction. Roberta hadn't been saying much after the other girls had finished, but JoJo hoped to be able to read her face and get a sense of how Roberta thought she had done.

"That was flawless," Roberta said a moment later. "Well done, JoJo."

JoJo grinned at the praise and walked back to the side of the room, an extra bounce in her step.

They spent the rest of Wednesday's class learning the middle part of the routine, and JoJo was happy to be partnered with Jamilla. Roberta broke up the Queen Bs, putting Belle with two of the ballerinas, and Bahi and Bree with Michelle. JoJo felt bad for the ballerinas

Belle was partnered with, and soon it was clear that Belle was up to her usual tricks. A few times JoJo and Jamilla heard Belle laughing at the other dancers or picking apart what they were doing, though she was always quick to act sweet and supportive whenever Roberta was nearby. JoJo did her best to tune it all out.

As Jamilla and JoJo took a quick water break, their attention was drawn to the corner of the room where Bree, Bahi, and Michelle were practicing together. JoJo wasn't sure what had just happened, but it seemed like Michelle must have mastered something she'd been struggling with, because Bree was clapping, and Bahi was saying, "Yessss! That was perfect!"

JoJo smiled as she watched the exchange— it was nice to see the Queen Bs supporting another dancer—but a moment later the smile faded from her face as Belle stormed over to where the other two Queen Bs were. JoJo couldn't hear everything Belle said—she was smart enough to keep her voice down so Roberta wouldn't overhear it either—but whatever it was, JoJo could tell it wasn't nice. Belle walked away, a satisfied smirk on her face.

"Maybe we should put the cupid cutout in the middle of the room to remind a certain someone about love and kindness," Jamilla whispered, gesturing to the paper cupid and winking at JoJo. "Although I think poor cupid would have his work cut out for him with Belle!"

JoJo giggled and took a gulp of water. She was so glad to be partnered with Jamilla. Jamilla was definitely someone who knew how to rise above it all.

JoJo walked into class on Friday excited to learn the last part of the routine. In honor of the fact that it was finally February— Valentine's month!—JoJo had dressed in red, white, and pink.

As she dropped off her things in her cubby, Bahi called out to her from the other side of the break room. "Great minds think alike, JoJo," Bahi said, grinning and gesturing to her own red-and-pink outfit.

"Well, it is officially February now!" JoJo exclaimed, smiling back.

"Aw, I wish I had gotten the memo to dress all festive!" Bree joked. "But my shirt is pink, so that kind of counts, right?"

"Bree, maybe you should worry less about what you're wearing and more about your dancing!" Belle snapped before stomping out of the break room. Bree and Bahi exchanged uncertain glances and then headed out after her.

"See you out there, JoJo," Bahi said. But all the enthusiasm was gone from her voice.

JoJo sighed and prepared herself for whatever the day's class would bring.

The dancers spent the first half of the class broken into smaller groups again, but this time Roberta changed the groups around several times to mix things up. JoJo had to work with Belle just once, but luckily it was for a brief time, and Belle focused on dancing and didn't say anything mean. Still, JoJo was relieved to switch partners. She had a hard time relaxing around Belle, though she enjoyed working with all the other dancers. She realized she could learn a little something from each of them and hoped that each of them felt as if they learned a little something from her.

"Maybe try raising your left hand after the shuffle like you did the first time," JoJo was saying to Bahi, whom she was currently partnered with. "That looked really good."

"Like this?" Bahi executed a few steps while JoJo watched. "Yeah, you're right, that feels better. Thanks!"

"No problem!" JoJo walked over to Bahi. "Now let's see if we can—"

Just then, the sound of Belle's laughter rang through the room. Most of the dancers stopped what they were doing and looked over to where Belle was practicing with Jamilla and Emily, one of the other ballerinas.

"Oh, sorry," Belle said when she realized all eyes were on her. "I didn't mean to laugh so loud. But that was just so funny!"

From the look on Emily's face, JoJo could tell that Emily had not been trying to be funny. Belle was making fun of her. Roberta walked to the front of the room and briskly announced that the groups were changing. JoJo ended up partnered with Bree and Lindsay, both of whom she'd already been partnered with earlier.

"Ugh!" Lindsay sighed in frustration. "I don't know what's wrong with me this afternoon! Maybe I really don't belong in this class!"

"Of course you belong here!" JoJo said firmly. She wondered if Belle had made Lindsay feel that way. "You were doing it perfectly earlier. Just take a deep breath and try again. It'll come back to you."

"Yeah, you got this!" Bree cheered.

"OK, here goes." Lindsay nodded in determination.

A few moments later, JoJo and Bree clapped excitedly after Lindsay nailed the combination perfectly.

"Thanks, you guys!" Lindsay said, taking a bow. "That felt really good. Now you two run through the whole middle and end part together while I watch!"

"Oh, I don't know if I'm ready," Bree said nervously. "I mean, talk about not belonging here. I mess up more than anyone."

"Let's just try!" JoJo said. "It's totally fine to make mistakes—just relax and let go."

Bree took a deep breath and nodded. "Okay, let's do this!"

"One, two, three," JoJo counted. The two girls danced in perfect unison and sailed through the entire second part of the routine. When they were finished, they grinned at each other and exchanged high fives while Lindsay clapped.

"That was literally the best I have ever done that part!" Bree exclaimed.

"You were awesome!" JoJo tucked a loose strand of hair behind her ear. "We looked pretty good together, didn't we?"

"You sure did!" Lindsay nodded. "That was flawless. You guys really dance well together. Too bad the solo isn't a duet!"

JoJo and Bree grinned happily at each other. The three girls decided it was a good time to take a quick water break and headed into the kitchen.

"JoJo, I meant it when I said that's the best I've ever done that part," Bree said quietly as she and JoJo sipped water. "I really like dancing with you. You're so good, and I just feel more . . . confident . . . when I'm with you."

"Thank you—that's a really nice thing to hear," JoJo said earnestly. "I think you are super talented, Bree." JoJo paused to refill her water cup. "Can I give you some advice, though?"

Bree nodded.

"Believe in yourself. You made it into this workshop because you're good. You're better than good. You belong here. You have to remember that and own it!"

"Own it," Bree repeated, a slight smile on her face. "Thanks, JoJo."

Bree, JoJo, and Lindsay were just about to head back to work when Roberta announced it was time for everyone to take a break. As the rest of the girls made their way into the kitchen area, JoJo could feel the tension coming off the other dancers in waves. Several of them looked upset, and they all looked lost in thought as they stood off on their own, not laughing and joking the way they usually did during break time.

"I guess everyone is stressed about the solo," Belle announced loudly as she looked around the room. When no one said anything, she walked over to Michelle and said in a loud whisper, "Roberta's probably regretting some of the selections she made for this workshop, and—"

Before she could complete her sentence, Michelle walked away. JoJo sighed. She couldn't believe the way Belle was acting. She was sure that the reason the dancers looked so discouraged was because of the way Belle had been putting everyone down all week. Michelle had been right when she'd said that drama like this was exhausting. It was exactly the sort of thing JoJo had been talking about in her hit song "Hold the Drama." Only one question remained: What could be done about it?

JoJo knew one thing for sure. Belle was probably being negative because she felt insecure or because someone else had bullied her before. JoJo couldn't fix that—not now, anyway—but she *could* make sure Belle's drama stopped hurting other people. The dancers needed some positive energy to offset Belle's negative energy. Maybe some of it would even rub off on Belle! JoJo was determined to make things right. She wanted to get the solo, but she wanted to get it because she earned it, not because the other dancers were too upset to perform.

The rest of the class passed quickly. JoJo did her best to be positive with the girls she was partnered with, and she felt like she was making a difference. Emily, the ballerina who had been struggling so much earlier in the day, sailed through the routine almost perfectly at the end of class and was so excited that she hugged JoJo.

Roberta called the dancers together before the end of class. "I have two announcements," she said in her low, husky voice. The room went so silent, you could hear a pin drop. "First, the date of our performance has to change due to a scheduling conflict with the arts center. It will now take place on February 16, the weekend *after* Valentine's Day."

JoJo almost couldn't believe her ears. February 16? She was going to be away that weekend. That meant she couldn't participate in the performance. Which meant she was out of the running for the solo. Her heart sank.

"Second, from now on," Roberta said as JoJo tuned back in, "there will be no commentary between dancers about anyone's performance. No critiques, no suggestions, nothing. You are each in competition with yourself only, to be the best dancer you can be. I am disappointed by what I've seen going on here between some of you, and I will not tolerate it. Are there any questions?"

Belle raised her hand. "What if we have a *compliment* for someone?"

JoJo saw some of the other dancers exchange looks. Belle had not had a kind comment to say to anyone since the workshop began. In fact, it was pretty obvious that Roberta was reacting to all of Belle's criticisms!

"No commentary," Roberta repeated firmly, her jaw clenched. "That includes compliments. Am I clear?"

JoJo and the others nodded. Roberta was crystal clear.

CHAPTER 7

It was Saturday night, and the Valentine's Day sleepover was under way. The girls had already had a special dinner inspired by the pancake breakfast JoJo had eaten at the diner with her mom on the morning of her first workshop class. They used even more chocolate syrup and whipped cream and had added chocolate chips to the batter, which really put the pancakes over the top.

"These might not *look* as perfect as the ones at the diner, but they taste every bit as delish!" JoJo had declared. Sure enough, their hearts were just a teeny bit crooked, and their strawberry roses weren't quite as flawless as the ones from the restaurant, but once they added powdered sugar to their plates, they'd never have known the difference!

Now they had all headed into JoJo's basement, one of JoJo's favorite spots in the house. The finished basement had a big-screen TV, comfy furniture, and plenty of arcade games, which made it a perfect hang-out spot when JoJo or Jayden had their friends over. Knowing that they would be spending a good part of their evening down there, JoJo had decked out the place in Valentine's Day decorations. Pink and red streamers dangled from the ceiling, and paper hearts with sayings like "Be Mine" and "I Heart You" covered the walls, but JoJo's absolute favorite decoration was a giant cardboard cupid she'd found that looked just like the one Roberta had in the studio, only about ten times the size—it was bigger than life-size! JoJo had attached a string to the jumbo cupid and dangled him from the highest part of the ceiling. The overall effect was that he was flying over the room with his bow and arrow drawn. It was equal parts hilarious and adorable.

"Oh! That is the biggest baby I've ever seen!" Grace exclaimed as soon as she reached the bottom of the stairs.

"Ha, I was hoping that would be the first thing you noticed when you came down here!" JoJo laughed. "It's cupid! Check out his bow and arrow!"

"He's kind of hard to miss!" Kyra agreed. "It looks so cute down here! But is it okay that I'm a little scared of giant cupid? We're not sleeping down here, are we?"

The other girls burst out laughing. "Aww, he comes in the spirit of love—I promise!" JoJo joked. "Take a selfie with him! You'll feel much better!"

A few minutes later, after the girls had all taken selfies with the giant cupid, they settled on the couch to decide what to do next. "Anyone in the mood for a rom-com?" JoJo asked. "Or should we save that for later and listen to music now? Anyone feel like dancing?"

"Do you feel like dancing perhaps?" Miley asked, waggling her eyebrows.

"Always!" JoJo replied. "But why the face?"

"I'm hoping you'll show us the solo from your workshop! If we move the coffee table, will there be enough room for you to perform it?" Miley asked, pointing to a section of the basement that had mirrored walls. That area had been JoJo's dance studio when she was younger, but it had recently been converted to a man cave for her brother and father.

"I think so," JoJo said a moment later. "But I told you guys, I'm not even eligible for the solo anymore. Do you still want to see it?"

"Of course we still want to see it!" all three girls exclaimed in unison.

"Only if you insist." JoJo gave them a wink and sprang off the couch so quickly that BowBow yipped in protest. JoJo was thrilled her friends wanted to see the routine. After all, she'd worked so hard to learn it!

A few minutes later the girls had cleared space in the middle of the floor. JoJo did some quick stretches to warm up and then began dancing. Moments later, she'd completely lost herself in the routine. That happened to her when she was dancing—her mind would be totally focused on what she was doing, and the movements came as naturally as walking. Before she knew it, the routine was finished. JoJo took a bow and then scanned her friend's faces.

"That. Was. SO. GOOD!" Miley exclaimed, rushing in for a hug.

Kyra's eyes were huge, and her mouth was hanging open, and Grace was beaming while jumping up and down and clapping. "JoJo, I knew how good you were, but, wow! Just wow!" Grace said in amazement.

"What she said," Kyra said finally. "JoJo, I've seen performances on Broadway that didn't even look like that," Kyra breathed.

"I am so proud of you, girl," Miley said, untangling herself from the hug. "That cho- reography is out of this world, but I can tell you added so much of yourself to it. That was even *better* than I expected, and you know how much I expect from you!"

"Aww, thanks, you guys," JoJo said. She took a deep swig of water and plopped down on the couch. Kyra settled down at the other end of the sofa while Miley took the recliner and Grace settled into a beanbag chair. "I can't wait to keep practicing next week to make it even better. I really do feel like I've become a stronger dancer already."

"I think you have too," Miley said. "And that's saying a lot! It's just such a bummer that you can't be in the running for the solo," she added. "I'm sure you would have gotten it!"

JoJo shrugged. "It is a bummer I can't go for it, and I *was* pretty disappointed at first. But the more I thought about it, I realized that this experience is about so much more than just the solo. I'm holding my own against older dancers, and it feels really good to know how much I can push myself. All in all, it's been totally worth it!"

"I'm glad all the drama hasn't taken away from the experience," Grace said solemnly. Over their pancake dinner, JoJo had filled in her friends on what had been going on with Belle's bullying.

"Oh, don't get me wrong, the drama has not been fun," JoJo sighed. She bent over to give BowBow a lift so she could sit on the couch—the little teacup Yorkie was too small to jump that high. "But as you guys know, I am pretty good at tuning it all out. You have to—*won't let the haters get their way*, right?" She grinned as she sang a line from her famous song. "I just wish the other dancers were able to tune her out better. I can actually *see* Belle bringing people down, and it makes me so mad! This one girl, Bree, is so good. I think she actually has a great shot at the solo. But half the time she's messing up because Belle gets in her head."

As JoJo finished speaking, she noticed that Kyra looked uncomfortable. Her big brown eyes were downcast, and she was nervously fidgeting with the ends of her dark ponytail. "You okay, Kyra?" JoJo asked.

"Oh, well ..." Kyra looked up, and JoJo could see that her cheeks were red. "I just ... I was just thinking about how I acted over the summer when we all met and how mean I was to you, Grace. I still feel so horrible about that."

Grace sprang up from her beanbag chair and sat down on the couch next to Kyra.

"I've long since forgiven you," she said firmly. "We're besties now, and what's past is past, right, you guys?" She looked to JoJo and Miley, who both nodded.

"You're a great friend to all of us, Kyra," JoJo agreed. "And trust me, what Belle is doing at the workshop is, like, level ten! She's tormenting an entire class of dancers!"

"Still," Kyra said, looking relieved, "I'm so glad you guys gave me another chance."

"I know this sounds weird, but hold that thought!" JoJo said before racing from the room and up the stairs.

When JoJo returned a few minutes later, she was carrying a big red shopping bag. Miley had moved to the couch and was seated on the other side of Kyra. JoJo stood facing her three friends.

"JoJo. Spill it," Miley said. "What's going on?"

JoJo was so excited, she was bouncing up and down. "So, this whole conversation about friendship totally reminded me of the Valentine's surprise that I have for you. I was going to wait and give it to you later, but now just seems like the perfect time."

Then JoJo reached into the shopping bag and, one by one, pulled out the Candy Kisses she'd made for each of her friends. Dark and milk chocolates for Grace, who had braces and couldn't eat anything sticky, gummy everything for Kyra, and a mix of chocolates, bubble gum, and Sour Patch Kids for Miley.

"Our favorite candies in cute, decorated bags?" Grace exclaimed as she eyed the treats. "This is the best thing ever!"

"The candy isn't even the best part," JoJo explained as she handed each girl her candy-gram. "I'm calling them Candy Kisses, and there's a special, personalized message inside.

It's a candy kiss from me to you, because I love you guys!"

"Aww, group hug!" Miley exclaimed a moment later. The three girls jumped off the sofa and circled around JoJo, giving her a big, four-way, best-friend hug. JoJo's heart swelled with happiness, all of the drama and disappointment from the workshop totally forgotten.

A few hours later, the girls were settled on JoJo's bedroom floor in their sleeping bags. Jessalyn popped her head into the room after gently knocking on the door. "You girls all set in here?" she asked. "Does anyone need an extra blanket or pillow?"

"I think we're good," JoJo replied. "We're wiped out! We might fall asleep in record time tonight," she added, yawning.

"That would be amazing," Jessalyn said. "And the kitchen is about to close for the night, so speak now or forever hold your peace!"

The four girls laughed. "We ate so much candy after dinner that I might not ever eat again," JoJo said, which sent her friends into another round of laughter, Jessalyn joining in this time. "We're good."

"Sweet dreams, girls." Jessalyn gave JoJo a kiss on the head before shutting the bedroom door behind her.

JoJo turned off the lights and listened to her friends rustling around as they got comfy. A few minutes later, the sound of slow, steady breathing filled the room. At least two of her friends were already asleep.

"JoJo, are you still awake?" Kyra whispered into the darkness.

"Yep," JoJo whispered back. "What's up?"

"I just wanted to say thanks again for my Candy Kiss and for what you said in my note.

I feel so much better now. Your note really helped me. So thank you."

"You're welcome. I'm glad you liked it," JoJo replied softly.

"Oh, and, JoJo?" Kyra whispered again a moment later. "I'm positive all the girls in your class know what you're about. I could tell from the minute I met you how kind you were."

"Thanks, Kyra." JoJo was grateful for her friends and so glad she'd had the chance to tell them how she felt about them. If only she could tell the other dancers in her workshop how talented she thought they were. She knew most of them really needed to hear it. Roberta's new rule was going to make it tough, though.

Just as she was beginning to drift off to sleep, an idea popped into JoJo's head. She got so excited, she nearly squealed. If her friends had loved their Candy Kisses, her fellow dancers probably would too! Why not make Candy Kisses for the girls in her workshop? When JoJo drifted off to sleep a little while later, she had a smile on her face.

CHAPTER 8

"**M**om, would you mind picking me up a little later tonight from class?" JoJo asked. "I want to give out the Candy Kisses after everyone's left, so they'll be in their cubbies when they show up on Monday." JoJo had chosen to leave the Candy Kisses anonymous, so everyone would look at everyone else as a possible sender. It was perfect—with a rogue cupid on the loose, they couldn't accuse one another of anything but kindness!

It was Friday morning, and JoJo had spent all her free time the past week working on the Candy Kisses for the dancers in her workshop. Miley, Grace, and Kyra had been so excited about JoJo's idea that they had all gone candy shopping together, and the girls had even come over after school during the week to help JoJo write all the dancers' names in puffy paint and glitter on the plastic baggies.

"Sure." Jessalyn nodded. She sat down at the kitchen table, where JoJo was putting the finishing touches on the personalized notes for each dancer. "If you want, I can actually pick you up at the normal time, and we can leave and do an errand, then come back later to drop them off. That way you won't risk anyone seeing you. But you'd have to get Roberta's permission to do that."

"Oooh, sneaky—I like it!" JoJo laughed. "I'll check with Roberta, but I'm sure she will be okay with it. I just have one more to finish up, and then I'll be ready to go."

"Are you still struggling with Belle's?" Jessalyn asked.

One of the first things Miley had said after hearing JoJo's plan—in addition to saying what a great idea it was—was that it was going to be really tough to come up with something kind to say to Belle.

"Should Belle even *get* one?" Grace had asked.

At first, JoJo wasn't sure. On the one hand, Belle didn't really deserve a Candy Kiss. Not when she'd been so mean to everyone else. But on the other hand, JoJo definitely didn't believe in excluding anyone. Plus, she knew a lot of bullies were mean because other people had bullied them. JoJo thought about how much the Candy Kiss she'd given to Kyra had meant to her. A little kindness could go a long way. After giving it some thought, JoJo had decided that Belle would get a Candy Kiss too.

"I think I came up with the right thing to say to her in the note," JoJo said, handing her mom the square red card she'd been working on. On it JoJo had written: *This Candy Kiss is just for you! Your determination shines through every time you perform! You are an incredible dancer—wishing you lots of luck with this performance and your career!*

"I think that's really nice," Jessalyn said, taking it in.

"Thanks." JoJo took the card back and slipped it into the bag of candy with Belle's name on it. "I meant what I wrote—she is *really* determined, and she is an incredible dancer. And even though she's behaved badly throughout the workshop, I still wish her luck in her career."

"I think you're pretty incredible," her mom said, giving her a kiss on the head as she got up from the table. "And you make me proud every single day."

After class that day, JoJo lingered behind to talk to Roberta. She knocked on the door to Roberta's office, which was open, but JoJo didn't want to barge in uninvited.

"I hope you are coming to tell me you'll be able to audition for the solo after all," Roberta said as she looked up, waving JoJo in.

"I wish," JoJo said, taking a seat on the wooden chair across from Roberta. "But I can't reschedule. That event was planned a long time ago," JoJo said. "They're counting on me." When JoJo had told Roberta about her conflict, Roberta was very disappointed, but she'd understood.

"Of course." Roberta nodded in her firm way. "Commitments are very important, especially for a young person with a busy career. You are doing the right thing, though I hate to not have you be a part of our performance. You are a very special part of this workshop, JoJo."

"Thank you so much," JoJo said. "That really means a lot, coming from you. I've loved taking this workshop, and I've gotten so much out of it."

"I'm glad." Roberta smiled. "So tell me, what can I do for you?"

"Oh, I almost forgot!" JoJo laughed. "I wanted to ask if I can come back later this evening, after everyone has left. I have a little surprise for the other dancers I wanted to drop off without them seeing me. It's sort of a Valentine's Day thing."

"Like cupid?" Roberta looked thoughtful as JoJo nodded. "Hmmm. May I ask you a question about your surprise?"

"Sure." JoJo held her breath. She wondered if Roberta would ask her what the surprise was. JoJo didn't know how to explain the Candy Kisses without mentioning all the drama that had been happening behind the scenes. Roberta had noticed some of it but not all. What if Roberta said no?

"Is cupid giving a surprise to all the dancers in the class or just some of them?"

"Oh, all of them," JoJo assured her. "Everyone gets her own personalized surprise. I just want it to be anonymous."

Roberta held JoJo's gaze for a moment longer; then a warm smile spread across her face. "That's wonderful, JoJo. Of course you may proceed. The studio is open until eight this evening."

"Great. Thank you so much!" JoJo stood up and was about to leave when Roberta motioned for her to sit back down.

"JoJo, you haven't told any of the other dancers that you won't be participating in the performance, have you?"

"No," JoJo replied, shifting in her chair.

"Good. Thank you. I would appreciate it if you kept it to yourself a while longer."

"I—I was wondering," JoJo said hesitantly. She took a deep breath and cleared her throat. "I was wondering why I can't say anything. If you wouldn't mind telling me, that is."

"The other girls push themselves harder because of you," Roberta said simply. "They know you are one of the top dancers in the class, and they work harder to match you. I know it's not an easy position to be in, especially being the youngest in the class, but I can tell that you are well equipped to deal with competition, as well as what it brings out in some people."

JoJo nodded. "Thanks for being honest with me," she said.

"Of course," Roberta replied. "Good luck with your cupid surprise later!"

CHAPTER 9

On Monday afternoon, the Candy Kisses were waiting in everyone's cubbies when they arrived, just where JoJo had left them on Friday after class. When JoJo walked into the break room to drop off her things, Lindsay, Michelle, and Jamilla were huddled together, sharing the contents of their bags with each other and giggling. JoJo smiled to herself when she saw how happy the girls looked.

Even Michelle, who had seemed so tense lately, was grinning from ear to ear.

"Hey, JoJo, wait until you see the surprise waiting for you in your cubby!" Lindsay called, waving as JoJo came in. "We all got these adorable bags called Candy Kisses from an anonymous cupid. It's definitely someone from our workshop, because the notes are each so personal!"

"Yeah, let's see what yours says," Michelle said.

"Oh—I . . ." JoJo tried to think fast. She hadn't thought to make a fake Candy Kiss for herself! If she opened her cubby in front of the other dancers, and they saw she didn't have one, they might figure out that she was the anonymous cupid! Crossing her fingers behind her back, she tried to sound casual as she said, "I already got mine and ran it out to the car for my mom to take home, so I wouldn't be tempted to eat all the candy during break!" JoJo let out a relieved breath as the other girls nodded. "But the note was nice," she added, turning to place her backpack in the cubby.

As JoJo hurried to put her things away and prepare for class, Michelle walked over to her and leaned against the wall of cubbies. "So your note was nice?" She smiled, giving JoJo a wink.

"Um . . . yeah," JoJo said. She had a feeling Michelle had figured things out, so she decided to change the subject. "Just two more classes before the big auditions!" she exclaimed, removing her dancing slippers and water bottle from her backpack. "Do you feel ready?" JoJo sat down on the bench to change her shoes, happy for an excuse to avoid Michelle's gaze.

"I think so," Michelle replied. "I don't think I'm going to get the solo," she added. "I mean, don't get me wrong—I'm going to dance my heart out for it—but I know I'm not the best dancer in this class. That would probably be you."

"Thank you for saying that, but everyone in this class is amazing," JoJo replied, and she meant it. As nice as it was to hear that Michelle thought JoJo was that good, JoJo didn't think one dancer could be picked out as the very best in the class. "Every dancer here is fantastic! I feel like I've learned from everyone."

"Me too." Michelle nodded. "But just so you know, I'm bringing my A game! I really am going to do my best to nab the solo!"

"You should!" JoJo laughed as she stood up, and the two girls walked out of the break room together.

That Monday's class was the best one of the entire workshop. The other dancers seemed relaxed and happy. Even Belle kept her commentary to herself. Most of the dancers had learned the whole routine, and JoJo couldn't wait to see who was going to nab the solo.

At the end of class, the dancers were all in the break room packing up their things and chatting.

"Cupid complimented me on my flexibility," JoJo overheard Emily saying to Jamilla. "I've always thought that was my greatest strength, but it's really nice to hear it from someone else."

"Definitely." Jamilla nodded. "Mine talked about how graceful I am, which I love hearing. I'm totally going to focus on that for my audition. I might not be able to do all the fast steps perfectly, but I know I'll look graceful while I try."

As JoJo listened to the other dancers happily chattering about their Candy Kisses and Wednesday's audition, all she could think was, *Mission accomplished.*

"So today's the big day!" It was Wednesday afternoon, and JoJo and Jamilla were in the break room. "Are you nervous about auditioning for the solo?"

"About that ..." JoJo looked around the room. None of the other dancers was there, and she wondered if it was okay now to tell Jamilla that she wasn't auditioning. But just then, Roberta walked into the room.

"JoJo, may I speak with you for a minute?" Roberta asked.

JoJo nodded. "Good luck out there," she whispered to Jamilla as she followed Roberta into her office.

"JoJo, I wanted to ask if you might like to help me judge the auditions," Roberta said. "You've worked so hard in this workshop, I'd like for you to still be involved in the performance in some way. What do you think?"

"I'd be honored," JoJo replied. "Thank you."

JoJo and Roberta walked out of her office together. JoJo could hear the nervous chatter and laughter of the other dancers. The pre-audition energy in the room was electric! Roberta started to walk to the front of the room to gather the dancers around, but then she realized she'd forgotten her clipboard and headed back to her office.

"I wonder what that little private pow-wow was all about," Belle loud-whispered to Bree. "I bet she's going to tell us that JoJo already has the solo . . ." Belle's voice trailed off as Bree walked away from her and went to stand on the other side of the room.

"Excuse me, did you just walk away from me?" Belle demanded of Bree.

Suddenly the room was so quiet, you could hear a pin drop. JoJo's heart sank as she realized that Belle was going to start an argument with Bree just before the auditions were set to begin—and no one needed that kind of drama! The dancers were nervous enough already.

But to JoJo's surprise, Bree just smiled and said, "Yeah, I guess I did. No offense, Belle, but I don't want to deal with your drama right now. I don't want to gossip about JoJo, or anyone else for that matter. I just want to rock my audition, so I'm gonna stand over here and focus on that." Then she looked around the room at all the faces of the other dancers. "Good luck, everyone!"

JoJo held her breath to see what would happen next, and she was so happy when everyone started chatting again as if nothing had ever happened.

Moments later, Roberta returned, clutching her clipboard. She walked to the front of the room and motioned for the dancers to gather around her. "JoJo Siwa will not be able to join our performance on Saturday evening due to a prior commitment she agreed to before the workshop began. Therefore, she will not be eligible for the solo."

JoJo felt nine pairs of eyes on her but kept her own gaze straight ahead, on Roberta.

"I have asked JoJo to join me as a judge today, something I believe she deserves, because she continued to come here and give this workshop her all, even after she knew she couldn't perform with us or be eligible for the solo. That is the kind of dedication one needs to succeed, and the mark of a true competitor!"

With that, Roberta motioned for JoJo to join her at the front of the room. The dancers dispersed to go change—they were going to audition in their costumes. JoJo couldn't wait to see her fellow dancers all dressed up. The auditions were about to begin!

CHAPTER 10

Jamilla was up first. She looked fantastic in her red leotard and flowing red skirt, but what JoJo almost couldn't believe when she saw it was that Jamilla had a big red bow in her hair! She gestured to the bow and winked at JoJo before she began. She danced her heart out, and JoJo had to stop herself from jumping out of her seat to applaud when she was finished.

Michelle went next, and JoJo couldn't believe it when Jamilla paused to remove the bow from her hair and hand it to Michelle, who fastened it in her own hair. JoJo held her breath through Michelle's performance, and her heart soared when Michelle made it perfectly through the one spot in the routine that had given her some trouble throughout the workshop.

By the end of the auditions, eight of the nine dancers had worn the red bow in her hair—Belle was the only one who didn't—and JoJo felt overwhelmed by the gesture her fellow dancers had made. She knew that by each of them wearing a JoJo bow in her hair, it was their way of making *her* a part of their auditions.

All nine girls danced beautifully, but to JoJo, one dancer's performance really stood out. She wondered if Roberta would agree. JoJo gathered her thoughts as she followed Roberta into her office so they could discuss who deserved to get the solo.

"Well, what are you thinking?" Roberta asked moments after closing the door.

"I thought everyone did a fantastic job, but one dancer stood apart from the rest for me. She made the solo her own in a really special way, and she gets my vote . . ."

JoJo told Roberta the dancer she had in mind, and Roberta smiled and nodded. "My thoughts exactly, JoJo. I'm glad we agree! And kudos to you for having such a keen judge's eye!"

JoJo felt like she was walking on air as she and Roberta made their way out of the office. She was super excited for the dancer they had chosen but also really proud of herself for having such a good eye for judging.

Roberta gathered the girls around and announced that the dancer who had won the solo was . . . Bree!

Bahi, Jamilla, and the other ballerinas gathered around Bree to congratulate her. Belle stood off to the side, scowling, but JoJo was relieved when Belle didn't say anything. After all, this moment was all about Bree!

"You totally earned it!" Michelle told Bree, giving her a hug. "After I saw you perform, I really hoped you would get it. That was a gold-medal performance!"

"Thank you so much," Bree said, her eyes shining with happy tears. Then she took a step away from Michelle and went over to thank JoJo and Roberta for choosing her.

"May I say something to the whole group?" Bree asked Roberta.

Roberta nodded, and Bree turned to face the dancers. She took a deep breath and smoothed down her skirt nervously. "Thank you all so much for your support. I can't believe I got the solo—it's such an honor to be chosen, because you all are so talented—and I promise to do my best and make you all proud at the performance."

The dancers cheered and applauded, and a wide, happy grin broke across Bree's face at their obvious show of support. "I think most of you know I struggled a bit throughout this workshop . . ." Bree's voice trailed off as she looked at the ground for a moment. Then she took another deep breath and continued, her voice strong. "I learned so much during my time here, but the best lesson I learned was to believe in myself. The Candy Kiss I got on Monday really meant a lot to me. So I just wanted to say thank you to whoever the anonymous cupid is."

For the second time that afternoon, JoJo felt several pairs of eyes on her, but she pretended not to notice and stayed focused on Bree, who let her gaze rest on JoJo for a quick moment before continuing. "Cupid told me that she loves when I dance like no one is watching. She said when I do that, I'm one of the best dancers she's ever seen. And if my Candy Kiss came from the person I *think* it came from, I know she's seen a lot of great dancers! So that made me feel pretty good." Bree winked, and all the other dancers giggled. "I really needed to hear that. So thank you, Cupid, whoever you are—for letting me know you believed in me. It made all the difference."

As everyone gave Bree one more round of applause, JoJo felt so happy, she thought she might burst. Few things felt as good as making someone else feel special, and knowing that her Candy Kiss had made such a difference for Bree was an incredible feeling.

"Oh, and one more thing!" Bree said suddenly, holding up a hand. The dancers quieted back down, waiting to hear what Bree would say next. "My name is actually Gabrielle, not Bree. So if you guys could call me Gabrielle instead of Bree from now on, that would be great. Thanks!" With that, she smiled shyly and walked from the center of the room. The other dancers gave her one more round of applause. JoJo clapped extra hard for Bree—Gabrielle—because she was so proud of her. And to make the moment even sweeter, JoJo thought that Bree had handled the situation perfectly—she had stood up for herself without calling Belle out.

The dancers drifted apart, some heading into the break room to change out of their costumes and others lingering around the kitchen to talk about the upcoming performance.

Just as JoJo was about to catch up with Jamilla in the kitchen, Gabrielle and Bahi approached.

"I just wanted to say thank you again," Gabrielle said, touching JoJo's arm.

"Don't thank me." JoJo patted Gabrielle on the shoulder. "You did all the work! You danced your heart out and earned the solo!"

"She's right, Bree." Bahi nodded. "I mean, Gabrielle. Sorry—that's going to take some getting used to! But you were fabulous, and you should *own* it!"

Gabrielle grinned. "Well, I just wanted you to know that I'm really glad I met you, and I hope we can keep in touch."

"That would be great," JoJo replied.

"Great!" Gabrielle grinned. "Now I have to go text my mom and tell her that I got the solo!"

As Gabrielle walked away, Bahi turned to JoJo. "I'd like to keep in touch too. Do you have any plans tomorrow night for Valentine's Day? Maybe we can all hang out?"

"By 'we,' do you mean the Queen Bs?" JoJo asked uncomfortably.

"Well, no, I was thinking me, you, and Gabrielle," Bahi explained. "I don't think Gabrielle wants to hang out with Belle anymore, and, um . . ." Bahi's voice trailed off, and now it was her turn to look uncomfortable. "Judging from Gabrielle's announcement, I think the Queen Bs are no more." Bahi paused, seemingly to try to choose her next words carefully. "JoJo, I know you probably don't understand why I'm friends

with Belle, but she can be really nice outside of the workshop, and, well, I know deep
down she cares about me. It's kind of hard
to explain, but she's my friend even though I
don't always love the way she acts."

"I actually have plans tomorrow night
with my best friends," JoJo replied, remem-
bering that she, Miley, Kyra, and Grace had
made plans to get together. "But for the
record, you can be friends with whoever you
want to be, and you don't have to explain it
to me. I'm glad Belle is a good friend to you,
and I would never hold it against you. You do
you, right?"

"That's right!" Bahi grinned in relief.

"But rain check on the three of us getting together," JoJo added. "We should invite
Michelle and Jamilla too!"

And with that, the girls headed into the
break room, where all the rest of the dancers

had gathered. JoJo looked at the happy, smiling faces around her and thought how very glad she was that the workshop had ended on such a positive note. The dancers had all grown in their own way from the workshop experience. And in the end, that was what mattered most.

CHAPTER 11

It was after school on Valentine's Day afternoon. Miley, Grace, and Kyra had just arrived at JoJo's house for their "Valentine's Day Party Take 2."

"That might be the most adorable shirt ever, and so perfect for today," JoJo was saying to Grace, who was sporting a pink long-sleeved tee that said *I Heart Unicorns*. The heart was red sequins, and the word *Unicorns* was in a fancy pastel rainbow script.

"Kyra gave it to me!" Grace beamed. "'Cause unicorns are my true love!"

All the girls had dressed up for Valentine's Day in some way. JoJo's bow was pink with red hearts. It matched perfectly with her over-sized pink sweater and leggings with little red hearts on them. Miley was dressed in head-to-toe red, her nails painted in ombre glitter shades of pink to red, and Kyra had woven red and pink ribbons through her side braid and was wearing dangling, heart-shaped earrings. JoJo loved that each of her friends had her own style, from Grace's love of all things uni-corn, to Miley's love of glitter and Kyra's now-signature hairdo of a thick, glossy side braid.

"It's too bad Jacob couldn't make it," Kyra said a moment later. "Bummer he had to study."

"Yeah, he was really worried about this history test he has tomorrow," Miley sighed.

"You guys know how he gets about that stuff! But he said he'll join us for sure next time."

JoJo glanced at the clock and realized they had a few hours to kill before dinner. Nothing like a pre-dinner sweet treat! "Who wants ice cream?" she asked, leaping up from the sofa to sprint into the kitchen. She assumed her friends would be right behind her. After all, her friends loved ice cream as much as she did! "We have strawberry, mint chip, cookies and cream, rocky road . . . and I think I even see some birthday cake explosion back there. *Hello? Anyone?*" JoJo closed the freezer door and looked around for her friends, but she was all alone in the kitchen.

"Um, guys?" she called, laughing. "Hello? Is this some sort of Valentine's Day prank? 'Cause if it is . . ."

Before JoJo could finish her thought, her three best friends strolled into the kitchen, each with her hands behind her back.

"We have a surprise for you!" Miley sang out.

"Oh!" JoJo jumped up and down. "What is it?" JoJo *loved* surprises. "Do I need to close my eyes?"

"No, you can keep them open." Grace laughed. "Maybe just sit down at the table."

JoJo practically ran to the table and took a seat, looking at her friends expectantly.

Miley and Grace nodded to Kyra, who began speaking. "We all loved our Candy Kisses so much that we got together and each made you one." Kyra held out a pink plastic bag she'd been holding behind her back. "Mine is filled with sweet chocolates, because you've been such a sweet friend to me." She handed the bag to JoJo. "You can read the card later," she added.

Next came Grace, who held out a white bag with red hearts and unicorns drawn on it. "Mine is filled with licorice ropes, because you've taught me to be strong and to stand up for myself," Grace said. "And you can read my card later too."

Finally it was Miley's turn. She held out a light pink bag with maroon puffy hearts and stars and glitter on it—it was very Miley. "Mine is filled with all sorts of sticky candy like bubble gum and caramels and taffy, because, well, you're my best friend, and you're *stuck* with me! That's basically what my card says too, because you know how much I love you!"

All four girls burst out laughing.

JoJo sprang up from her chair, holding out her arms. "Thank you guys so much!" she cried, pulling her friends in for a group hug. "You are the best friends a girl could ever wish for!"

"No, JoJo, you are," Grace said as they pulled apart. "Seriously—you are so special to us, and we just wanted you to know that."

Just then, BowBow wandered into the kitchen and let out an excited little yip.

"Aww, she wants in on all the Valentine's Day love," Kyra cooed, bending over to scoop up the little pup.

"Oh, that reminds me ..." JoJo snapped her fingers and ran over to a kitchen cabinet. "I have a doggie kiss for BowBow!"

"Doggie kiss?" Grace replied, laughing. "What's that?"

JoJo returned holding a little baggie filled with chew-bones, dog treats, and a special heart-shaped doggie bow. "Well, I can't give BowBow people candy, but I can give her treats and chew toys! And a special Valentine's Day bow!"

Kyra handed BowBow to JoJo, who showed the little Yorkie her Valentine's surprise. BowBow sniffed the bag and let out a few excited barks as JoJo attached the pink heart-shaped bow to a tuft of fur on her head.

"Happy Valentine's Day, BowBow!" the girls cried, all taking turns giving BowBow a kiss. BowBow was happy to get all the kisses but even happier to get the treats!

Just then, Jessalyn came into the kitchen, a mischievous smile on her face. "Sorry to interrupt, girls, but now I have a surprise for JoJo. It's actually sort of a surprise for all of you! C'mon, grab your coats. We have to get in the car. We're going somewhere!"

"Wait, what?" JoJo asked. "Mom, what's the surprise?"

"It wouldn't be a surprise if I told you, now, would it?" Jessalyn laughed.

"C'mon, one hint!" JoJo cried, but her mom just shrugged and smiled. "Ugh, fine! But can BowBow come?"

"Actually, yes, she can! I checked!" Jessalyn replied.

"You had to check if BowBow was allowed to come?" JoJo cried, biting her lip. "That's sort of a hint. Hmmm . . ."

As the girls went to grab their coats, JoJo nudged Miley. "Do you have any idea what this is?" JoJo whispered.

"No idea," Miley replied, her eyes wide.

Everyone piled into the car, and about twenty minutes later, Jessalyn pulled into a circular driveway. JoJo had caught the name written in block letters on the mailbox, so she had an idea of *where* they were, but she had no idea *why*.

"Um, why are we here?" JoJo asked.

"I've been sworn to secrecy," Jessalyn replied. "Just go knock on the door!"

"Where are we?" Grace, Miley, and Kyra all cried in unison from the backseat.

JoJo hopped out of the car, BowBow in her arms, and opened the back door for her friends. "I'm actually not going to tell you guys, so I can wait and see the looks on your faces . . . even though I'm still not quite sure why my mom is bringing us here now!"

As JoJo and her friends walked up to the front door, JoJo's mind was racing a million miles an hour. Why had her mom dropped her and her friends off at Michelle Lee's house on Valentine's Day? Was Michelle expecting them?

A moment later, Michelle opened the door, grinning from ear to ear. JoJo noticed that Michelle had a red bow in her hair.

Before Miley, Grace, and Kyra could even grasp who was standing in front of them, Michelle pulled all four girls inside. JoJo was barely through the front door when she heard a loud chorus of "Surprise!"

As JoJo looked around the room, she saw all the girls from her dance workshop—even Belle—all with JoJo bows in their hair, and all cheering for her.

"Wait, I'm confused!" JoJo exclaimed a moment later. "It's not my birthday! What is going on?"

"We suspected you were responsible for the Candy Kisses, JoJo, so we asked Roberta," Jamilla said, stepping forward. "They meant so much to us! We asked your mom what we could do to thank you, and she told us Valentine's Day is one of your favorite holidays! So we thought we'd give a little love right back to you!" With that, Jamilla moved to one side and pointed to the dining room table, which was covered in colorful plastic baggies, all hand-decorated with hearts, glitter, musical notes, and all with JoJo's name on them. They were Candy Kisses from every girl from the workshop, to JoJo.

"Candy Kisses for our cupid!" Gabrielle whooped, and all the girls laughed.

"Hang on, I still don't know what you're talking about," JoJo said. Then, as she looked around the room at all the smiling faces of her friends, old and new, she realized it was okay to admit it. She'd made all her friends feel special, and now they wanted to make her feel special. And she was going to own it!

JoJo knew this was one Valentine's Day she would never, ever forget.

READ ON FOR A SNEAK PEEK FROM

JoJo & BowBow

THE POSH PUPPY PAGEANT

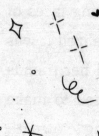

CHAPTER 1

"BowBow, no!"

JoJo Siwa didn't often say "no" to her cute, snuggly, fur-ball friend, but BowBow Siwa didn't often jump paw-first into their neighbor's slimy green koi pond!

BowBow gave JoJo a look that said, "You can't be mad at me!" Then she splashed her way back to the lawn, where JoJo stood waiting with her friend, Jacob.

"Careful, JoJo," Jacob said. "Don't let Bow-Bow get too close! She's all muddy."

But it was too late. BowBow trotted over and shook out her fur.

"Oh, BowBow," JoJo said to the stinky teacup Yorkie. "You smell terrible."

"Yeah, that pond is more for decoration than for swimming," Jacob said.

"Well I hope you have a garden hose, 'cause BowBow's gonna need one!"

JoJo scooped up BowBow in one hand and plugged her nose with the other while Jacob ran into the house. Soon he returned with a hose, some shampoo, and a handful of rags.

"I've never given a dog a bath before," said Jacob. "So I grabbed Oscar's gentle baby shampoo just in case."

"That's perfect," JoJo said. "You're the best! Now if only BowBow will stay still. . . ."

BowBow had other ideas. Soon Jacob and JoJo were both covered in soap!

"Phew," JoJo said a couple of minutes later. "I think we got all the pond muck out—we can set her down in the grass for a last rinse."

The two took turns squirting down Bow-Bow. Then Jacob aimed the hose at JoJo! By the time BowBow's bath was finished, all three were exhausted and happy.

"Maybe we should toss BowBow back in the pond," Jacob suggested. "That was fun."

"Don't even joke about it!" JoJo giggled.

"All that running around made me hungry," said Jacob, patting his stomach. "Want to grab a snack?"

The two walked through the sliding glass door into Jacob's kitchen. His mom was sitting at the counter with her laptop.

"Hey, kiddos," she said. "Looked like you were having fun out there!"

"BowBow jumped in the koi pond," JoJo told her. "But don't worry, she can swim."

"And don't worry, she doesn't like sushi," joked Jacob.

"Well I'm glad of that," his mom said. "How about some peanut butter on a rice cake for BowBow and some cookies for you two? Unless you want sushi, that is. I think we have a fishing pole around here somewhere...."

Jacob smiled and gave his mom a quick hug as he headed for the pantry.

"I'll leave you kids alone," Jacob's mom said, gathering her things. "Nice seeing you, JoJo!"

As the two kids and BowBow were chomping away, the doorbell rang.

"Must be Miley," Jacob told JoJo. "I texted her while we were outside."

Miley, Jacob, and JoJo had been best friends for years. They'd met in the neighborhood when JoJo moved in, and they'd quickly bonded.

Miley burst into the house without waiting for someone to let her in. "Hello?" She popped into the kitchen, her big smile warming JoJo.

"Mmmm my favorite. How did you know?" Miley slid onto a bar stool and grabbed a handful of cookies, then pulled out a purple, glittery notebook. JoJo leaned over her shoulder and read, "Spring Charity Event."

"What are you guys doing for your fund-raiser this year?" JoJo asked Jacob and Miley.

"That's actually why I asked Miley over," Jacob told JoJo. "We're allowed to team up with partners this year, and Miley and I got paired."

"Amazing," JoJo said. "You know I'm happy to help."

Every year, Jacob and Miley's school organized a charity fund-raiser. Any kids who wanted to participate could pitch an idea to the school for approval.

"Your bake sale last year was killer, Jacob," Miley told her friend. "Remember how fast you sold out of fudge pie?"

"Now how can we come up with something creative and fun again this year?" Miley drew her eyebrows together. "Oh!" she squealed, as BowBow's little nose touched her foot under the table. "I didn't see you there, BowBow." She stooped down and scooped up the dog, cuddling her close. "Mmmm, BowBow, you smell good. Did you just have a bath?"

Jacob and JoJo exchanged a look, then burst out laughing.

"We gave her one in the backyard," JoJo said. "It was an emergency situation."

"Really? You did an awesome job," Miley said.

JoJo looked up to see Miley staring at her with a gleam in her eye. JoJo knew that look! Miley's eyes only sparkled like that when she had a big idea. . . .

Then JoJo got it. "Miley, are you thinking what I'm thinking?" JoJo asked.

"What?" Jacob looked back and forth between the two of them. "What are you guys thinking?"

"A dog wash!" JoJo cried, just as Miley shouted, "A puppy spa!"

"Yes, that," they both said.

"It's perfect, Jacob," JoJo said to her friend. "Think how much fun we had today! People can drop off their pups, and we'll wash them up..."

"And maybe give them a little extra sparkle," Miley added.

"And then they'll pick them up at the end of the day."

"I know!" Miley looked up from her notebook. "When all the puppies are clean, we can do a puppy pageant to show off their new looks."

"And the winner will get an amazing prize," JoJo finished. "It's perfect!"

"I don't know," Jacob said, looking worried. "I'd have to ask my mom. She may not want all those dogs running around."

"Well then," JoJo said. "We have some convincing to do!"

More books available by JoJo Siwa!